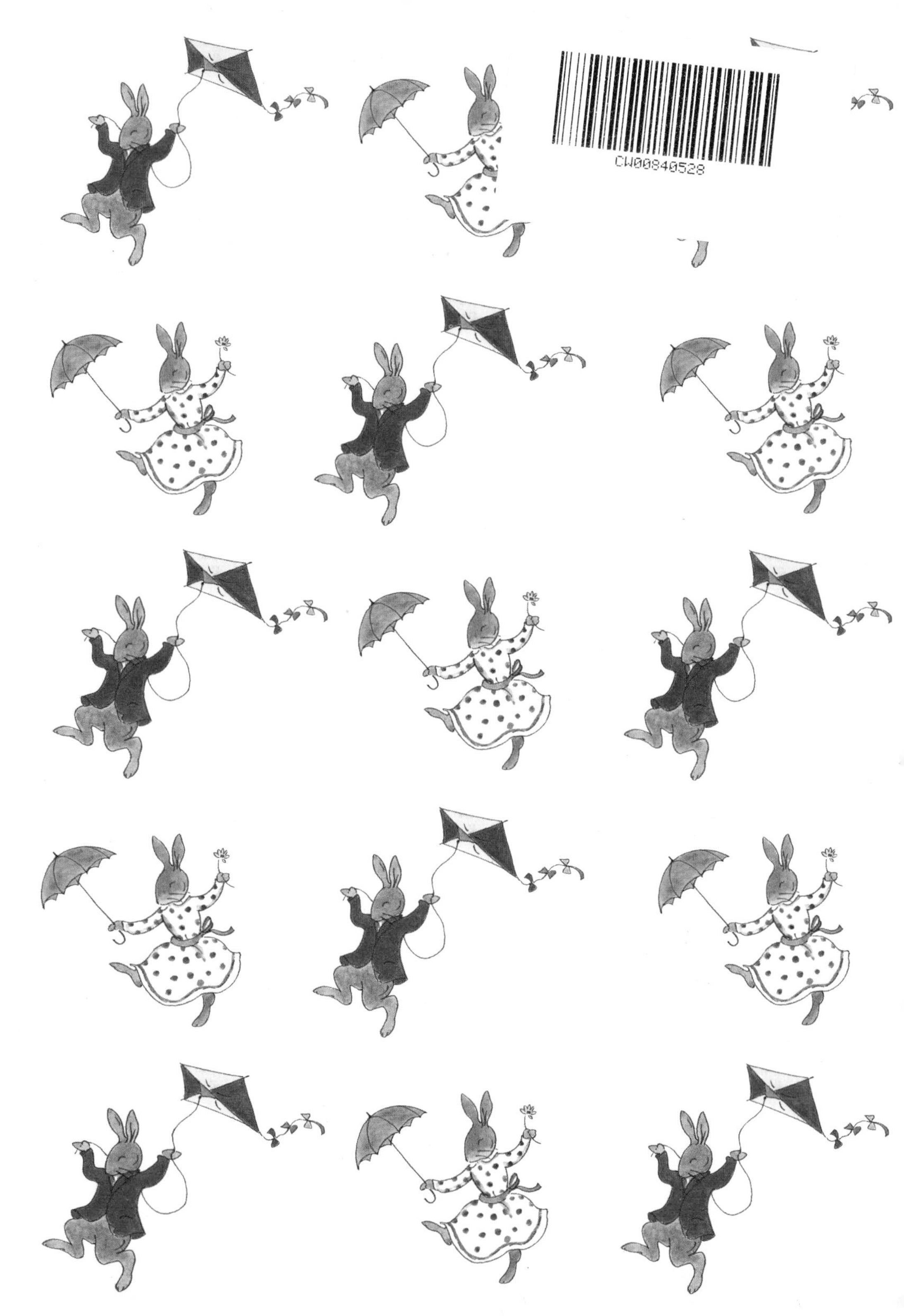

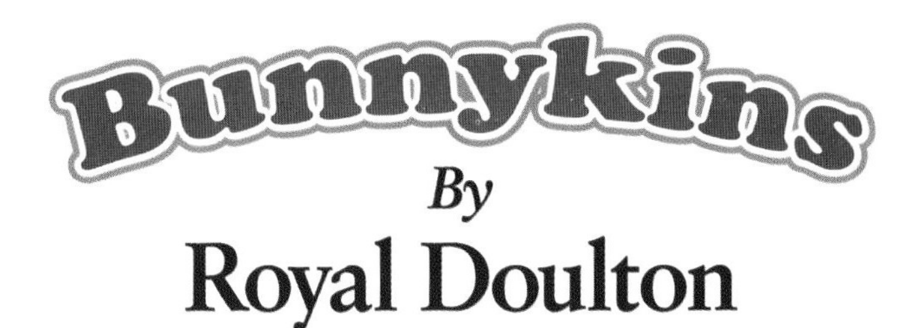

My First Stories

Manufactured under licence by small world creations ltd

for Bookmart Limited, Desford Road,

Enderby, Leicester LE9 5AD.

Printed in Italy

My First Stories

Written by Janet Brown
Illustrated by Frank Endersby

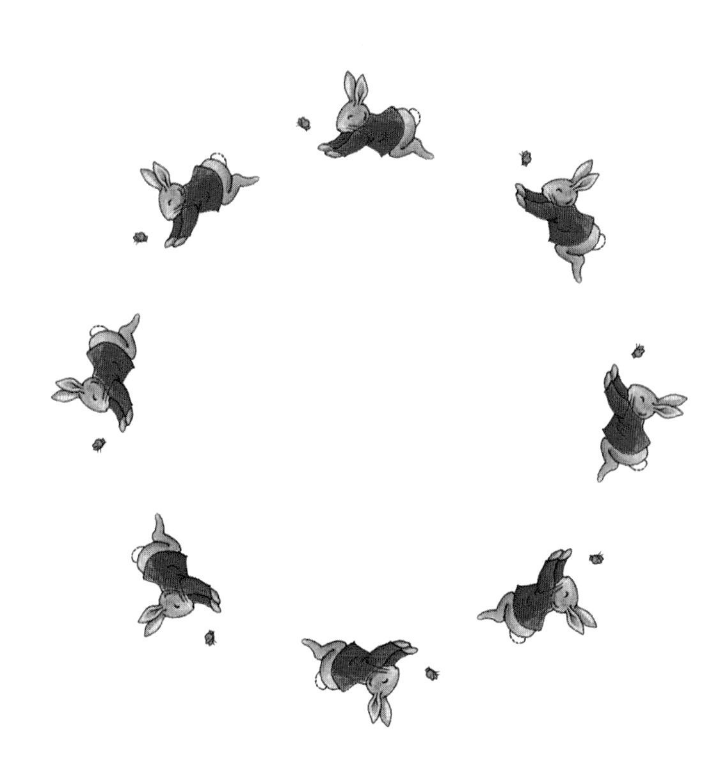

Contents

Susan Comes Second

Susan Comes Second

The Bunnykins children were very nervous. Every class in Hedgerow School had taken a test, and today they would get their results.

William was feeling rebellious because he knew he had not worked very hard. "I don't care what mark I get," he announced. "I'm going to be a postman like Grandad Whiskers, and Grandad told me he *never* worked hard at school."

POST

The twins didn't really care about tests - Harry was too busy practising his drums, and Tom knew he had done rather well. Polly was in the youngest class, so her test had been easy.

Only Susan was quiet. "I know you'll do very well," said Father comfortingly.

But that was the problem! Susan was a very clever bunny and she was so used to being top of her class that anything less just wouldn't do.

"What if I'm not top this year?" she thought. "The new girl in my class is very clever. What if she gets better marks than I do? Father will never forgive me!"

Susan walked to school with William. "Everyone knows you'll be top of the class again," he grumbled - and that didn't help Susan's feelings one bit!

In the classroom, Miss Harebell, the teacher said, "You've all done very well this year. I shall now read out your results."

And she began to list the names.

Susan's worst dreams came true - the new girl was top of the class, and Susan was only second! "Well done, Susan!" said Miss Harebell afterwards. "I can always count on you to do well."

But Susan was nearly in tears. Second place just didn't feel good enough.

"Congratulations," Susan mumbled to the new girl.

At the end of the day she ran home.

Through the windows she could see her brothers and sisters in the kitchen with Mother, showing off their results.

Everyone had done well, even William. Mother was looking very pleased.

Susan slipped into the garage to hide.

When Father came home, Mrs Bunnykins was waiting for him on the doorstep. "Susan hasn't arrived home yet," she said anxiously.

"Don't worry," said Father. He knew his eldest daughter very well. He went straight into the garage and pretended to start mending the kitchen clock.

Susan came slowly out of her hiding place.

"Hello," said Father, tinkering with his tools. "How was your day?"

Susan burst into tears. "I've got my results," she sobbed. "You're going to be very disappointed."

Father put his arms around her. "It can't be as bad as all that," he said. "You work very hard, Susan, and you're a clever girl. I don't care how badly you've done as long as you haven't been lazy or naughty."

"Really?" said Susan, looking amazed. "What if I told you I was bottom of the class?"

"Did you do your best?" asked Father.

"Yes," said Susan truthfully.

"Then I'd say good girl, I'm very proud of you."

Susan was silent for a minute. Then she said, "I didn't come bottom, Father. I came second. I wanted to come top. Everyone expected me to come top."

"No one can always be top of everything," said Father wisely. "You're not the only clever bunny in the world. But you are one of the most hard-working bunnies I know and, what's more, you're my special bunny, and I'm proud of you whether you come second, third or bottom of your class."

Inside Mother was waiting with a mug of hot chocolate.

"I hear you did very well," she said, kissing Susan. "And I also hear that you were very nice to the new girl who came top."

The Bunnykins had a special dinner that evening to celebrate everyone's results.

"I'm very proud of all of my children," said Father Bunnykins, beaming around the table.

Then he winked at Susan and added, "Although if William can do this well without really trying, I'd like to see what he can achieve with a little more effort!"

William looked at his feet in embarrassment. "I will try harder," he promised. "But we can't all be as clever as Susan."

Father's Big Surprise

Father's Big Surprise

One day Father Bunnykins heard Polly talking to her dolls.

"Poor Little Anne," said Polly. "Your bed is too small. And this chair is looking *very* shabby. Never mind, we'll have to make do."

Then and there, Father decided to make Polly some new furniture for her dolls.

That evening he went into his garage and began to work on his big surprise.

Father was finishing off a doll's cradle when he heard his neighbour, Mrs Bobtail.

There she was standing on her tippy-toes leaning over the fence. He sighed and wondered what William had done *this* time.

"I couldn't help noticing the light on in your garage," called Mrs Bobtail. "Whatever are you doing in there at this time of the evening?"

Mrs Bobtail was a kind soul but Father knew that she repeated everything she heard all over the village and, what was worse, she often got her facts wrong!

He very much wanted the dolls furniture to be a surprise for Polly, so he simply said, “I’m planning a little surprise, Mrs Bobtail. Good evening to you!”

And he returned to the garage.

Mrs Bobtail went back to her house in great excitement. That night she could hardly sleep for thinking about Mr Bunnykins surprise.

In the morning, she decided to share the news.

She put on her headscarf and went into the village.

The first person she met was Mr Baggins the postman.

"What news I have!" she told him, looking very pleased with herself. "Mr Bunnykins is planning a surprise for his family. But of course, I can't tell anybody what it is."

And she left Mr Baggins scratching his head and trying to guess.

Next, Mrs Bobtail went to see Mrs Humbug at the sweet shop.

"Great news!" said Mrs Bobtail. "My good friend and neighbour, Mr Bunnykins, is planning a big surprise for his family!"

"What kind of surprise?" asked kind old Mrs Humbug.

Mrs Bobtail paused for thought. "He's making something," she said at last. "Something mechanical. And judging by the noise, I would say it was something very big."

Mrs Bobtail was enjoying herself.

She left the sweet shop and went to find Mrs Velvetears in the toyshop.

But Mrs Velvetears had already heard the news. "The Bunnykins surprise!" she cried jumping up and down in excitement.

Mrs Bobtail was disappointed. It was her piece of news, and she wanted to tell it.

"This is the biggest surprise Little Twitching has ever seen," she sniffed. "It's a huge, mechanical, noisy invention, and I believe the whole village will be invited to come and see it when it's finished."

LITTLE
TWITCHING

Soon the whole of Little Twitching was talking about Mr Bunnykins' amazing invention.

Nobody knew anything about it but everyone pretended they did, and Mrs Bobtail went on adding more and more detail!

On Saturday morning all the new dolls' furniture was finished.

Imagine Father's surprise when he opened the garage door and found the whole of Little Twitching standing waiting in his garden!

"What's going on?" he asked in amazement.

"We've come to see your invention," explained Mr Baggins. "It was kind of you to invite the whole village to come and watch."

"There's no invention,"said poor Mr Bunnykins. "I've been making dolls' furniture for my Polly."

Shy little Polly burst into tears of excitement. "Dolls furniture!" she cried. "For me?"

She ran into the garage and everyone heard her squeals of delight. "Oh Father, it's all wonderful! Ella and Bella and Little Anne will be so grateful!"

"Whilst everyone's here," said Mother, "why don't we all have a nice cup of tea?"

Mrs Bobtail, who was feeling quite ashamed of herself, ran home to fetch some cake, and soon there was a huge teaparty on the Bunnykins' front lawn.

Everyone said such admiring things about Polly's new dolls furntiture that Father secretly felt rather pleased and proud of his surprise - even if it wasn't a huge, mechanical, noisy invention!

"That Mrs Bobtail could gossip the leaves off the trees," he said to Mother later.

But he made sure that the children didn't hear him!

Watch out, Reginald Ratley!

Watch out, Reginald Ratley!

William Bunnykins and Reginald Ratley were sworn enemies. Whenever Reginald saw William playing in the street, he would whisper to his friends and they would laugh and point.

It made William go hot all over. I'm sorry to say that, although William was a well-brought up bunny, he and his friends did exactly the same back to Reginald.

"I don't understand why you bother with Reginald," said Susan one morning as they were playing in the garden. "He's just a rude, silly bunny."

"He's a low-down rotter," said William with a fierce expression that he had been practising in front of the mirror. "He's a scoundrel. He thinks he's clever, just because he lives in a big house."

"He is clever," said Susan. "He's top of his class in every subject."

"That's because he's such a swot," said William, taking aim with his catapult and firing straight into the apple tree.

"Now William," said Mrs Bunnykins, standing on the doorstep with her hands on her hips.

"I won't have you using such language. You don't have to like him, but you must try and get on with him just the same."

"I don't see why," grumbled William.

That afternoon William and two of his friends, Adrian and Biffy, went into the nearby woods to build a tree-house where they could meet up to plan raids on Reginald and his gang.

The three friends found a perfect tree, with long flat branches close to the ground.

They worked for two hours, building walls and a roof.

Biffy hoisted their club flag to the top of the tree.

It was a warm, sunny day and soon they were all thirsty.

"I've had enough," said Adrian. "I'm going home to get some lemonade."

"Me too," said Biffy. "Come on, William."

"Nearly finished," said William. "You two go ahead."

William was all alone in the woods. It was very peaceful.

After a while he laid on his back in some moss, watching the sunlight flickering through the leaves.

Suddenly he heard someone calling for help.

The sound came from nearby and William recognised the voice - it was Reginald Ratley!

William suspected a trick. Here he was, all alone without his friends. Who knew what Reginald was planning?

But the voice came again. "Help! Help!"

Suddenly William could tell that this was serious. Reginald was in trouble!

Quick as a flash, William jumped to his feet and ran through the woods -

and there was Reginald, high up in the branch of a tree, with tears pouring down his face.

"What's the matter?" asked William.

"I'm stuck," cried Reginald. He didn't look brave or snotty any more. He looked frightened.

"Well why don't you just climb down?" said William sensibly.

"I'm scared of heights," said Reginald. "My friends made me climb up here and then they ran away. I pretended I was okay, but now they've gone and I can't get down."

Reginald may have been his sworn enemy, but William hated to see someone in trouble.

He climbed up to where Reginald was clinging to the branches .

"Right," he said firmly, taking control. "You must do as I say. Put your feet here and your hands here." Reginald did as he was told, crying all the time.

Soon the two enemies stood face to face at the bottom of the tree.

"Are you going to tell everybody?" asked Reginald fearfully. William shook his head.

"No," he said. "But now you owe me a favour. One day if I'm in trouble, then you must help me. And we're both sworn to secrecy."

They shook hands solemnly.

"You've got a super gang," said Reginald, feeling better now that he was safely on the ground. "It's quite fun being enemies, isn't it?"

William thought about it and realised it was true. What was the point of having a gang if there was no one to quarrel with?

Without Reginald and his pals there would be no raids, no point in practising the catapult, no one to make fun of.

William began to smile. "Everyone needs a good enemy," he agreed.

The two bunnies ran home. Afterwards Reginald continued to tease William, and William went on making fun of Reginald.

But secretly they both knew that, really, it was all just a game.

Bunnykins By The Sea!

Bunnykins By The Sea!

The twins had wanted to go to the seaside for a long as they could remember.

William and Susan had already been, and sometimes they would tell amazing stories about building sandcastles and collecting shells.

So on the Spring Bank Holiday when Father said, "I think it's Tom's and Harry's turn to decide where we should go for the day", there were no prizes for guessing what they said!

"The sea, the sea, the sea!" they yelled, hopping about in great excitement.

"The seaside it is," said Father, winking at Mother, who had already packed the picnic.

"Twins, help your mother clear away breakfast. William, you come and help me pack the car. Susan and Polly, can you find some big towels? We're leaving in ten minutes."

Soon they were all in the car. It was a long journey so they sang songs and played car games.

"Of course, the sea can be quite rough," said Susan, showing off a bit. "You've got to wear armbands in the water."

"And I don't suppose your sandcastle will be as big as the one I built last time," boasted William.

But the truth was that William and Susan were just as excited as Tom and Harry.

Suddenly the twins nudged each other and gave a huge yelp of delight.

"I can see something huge and blue!" cried Tom. "And it isn't the sky!" shouted Harry.

"It's the sea!" squealed Susan. "Hurray!"

The Bunnykins family stood on the shore and looked out to sea.

"The sand is so golden," sighed Polly.

"And the water is so blue," said Tom.

"Let's go swimming!" yelled William.

"Armbands first," said mother. The children changed into their swimming costumes and ran to the water's edge.

William rushed straight in, followed closely by the twins.

"It's f-f-freezing!" they shouted, splashing each other all over.

"Too cold for me," said Susan. She went back to Mother and Baby.

Polly was watching the boys. Father could see that she was nervous of the waves.

"Let's collect shells," he suggested, taking her hand. They paddled at the edge of the water and filled Father's sunhat.

The twins soon came out of the water and Mother wrapped them in a big towel.

"We're going exploring," they announced as soon as they were warm. "Shall we take Baby with us?"

The three bunnies wandered hand in hand through the rockpools. They found some crabs and little fish.

"Oooh!" squealed Baby, wiggling her feet in the warm pools. Tom licked his lips and found that they tasted of salt from the sea.

They felt the sun on their faces and the sand between their toes, and felt very happy.

At lunchtime everyone sat on the rug and ate the fish-paste sandwiches and jammy scones that Mother had packed in the picnic basket.

"I've got sand in my sandwich," grumbled Susan, pulling a face.

"It makes it taste better," said William.

"Well, twins," said Father, "what do you think of the seaside?"

The twins had their mouths full of food, but they nodded vigorously and their faces told Father how much they were enjoying themselves.

Then everybody helped to build an enormous sandcastle. Polly decorated the sides with pink shells, and the boys dug a large moat which soon filled with water. Baby chose a seagull's feather to stick in the top as a flag, and then they decorated the castle grounds with dried seaweed and bits of driftwood they found on the shore.

Later in the afternoon the tide began to rise and they watched the castle being washed away. Polly began to cry.

"Don't be sad," said William kindly. "This sandcastle was better than the one I built last time, and next time we'll make one that's even grander."

"And just think," said Father sensibly, "that if everyone's sandcastle lasted and lasted, there'd be no room left to play on the beach."

That night, six little bunnies were in bed and asleep by seven o'clock, exhausted by the sun and the sea air.

In their dreams they heard the swish of the waves and tasted salt on their lips.

Harry Makes Music

Harry Makes Music

Harry had two great ambitions in his life.

One of them was to play the drums in a band,

and the other was to sing with the school choir.

Tom preferred to practise his impersonations and plan tricks with William, but he was very encouraging.

"You should go and see the music teacher at Hedgerow School," he told his twin.

So Harry went to see Mr Brumpton the next morning. "I'd like to play the drums with the school band," he explained. "And I'd like to join the choir as well."

"That's a lot of work," said Mr Brumpton. "You may be better off choosing between them. But let's audition you first."

"Okay," Harry agreed, and then looked puzzled. "What's an audition?" he asked.

"It means you have to show me what you can do. The standard of music in this school is very high. We can't have just anyone playing and singing, you know," chuckled Mr Brumpton.

Harry felt very nervous. He had thought he could just join up. He hadn't realised there would be any tests!

"Right ho," said Mr Brumpton. "Let's try the singing first. I'll play a few notes on the piano, and you sing them back to me."

Mr Brumpton played five notes very slowly. Harry tried to sing the notes, but it came out all wrong. "Never mind," said Mr Brumpton kindly. "You're probably just nervous. Let's try again."

But Harry was not just nervous. He was tone-deaf - which means he couldn't tell one note from another, even when Mr Brumpton repeated them six times!

"Well, well," said Mr Brumpton, scratching his head. He could see how much Harry wanted to sing. "Never mind that. Just sing me a song."

Harry cleared his throat. This was better - now he could show the music teacher what he really could do!

He began to sing a lullaby in a loud voice. But he was completely out of tune - and because he was tone-deaf, he couldn't tell.

Mr Brumpton wanted to put his hands over his ears but, of course, he was too polite.

"Ahem!" he said hurriedly when Harry had finished. "Let's try the drums."

Harry sat at the drums and lifted the drumsticks.

They felt very comfortable in his paws. He began to play a gentle beat, and then built it up into a marvellous crescendo of cymbals and drum-rolls.

"Fabulous!" cried Mr Brumpton. "I've never heard such a talent! You must play with our band!"

Harry beamed and gave the cymbals an extra crash. Then he said enthusiastically, "And what about the choir?"

Mr Brumpton was a kind teacher and he had taught many bunnies in his lifetime.

He knew that if he told Harry that he couldn't sing, Harry would lose confidence and he might not want to play the drums anymore.

"Let's see," said Mr Brumpton, thinking quickly. "We really need you on the drums, you know Harry. And we've got a lot of rehearsing to do. What would you say to singing at the same time as playing the drums? That way we can use both of your talents."

Harry was delighted! He ran home and found his sister Polly in the bedroom, giving her dolls a tea party.

"Guess what," he told her. "They need me in the band *and* the choir, so I'll have to play the drums and sing at the same time!"

Polly was very impressed. "That must be awfully difficult," she said in admiration. "You must be very clever, Harry."

Tom was very impressed as well. "Well done!" he said, slapping Harry on the back. "I promise to come to every concert you do."

Mr and Mrs Bunnykins were very pleased, too.

"Harry is lucky he's got such a clever teacher!" chuckled Father, when he heard the news.

Of course, it was many years before Harry realised that the sound of drums completely drowned out his terrible singing voice. But by then he was a famous drummer, so it didn't really matter!

And do you know - every time that Harry performed in Little Twitching, Mr Brumpton was in the audience, clapping louder than anyone.

William Bunnykins, Magician

William Bunnykins, Magician

Father and Mother Bunnykins sat in the living room. Father had been in the office all day and was reading the newspaper. Mother was knitting. The children were nowhere to be seen but there was a lot of giggling and whispering coming from the bedroom.

"Are you nearly ready?" called Father.

"Two more minutes!" replied Susan in a muffled voice. There was a loud crash and Tom put his head around the door. "Nothing to worry about!" he said cheerfully.

Then Polly came into the living room. She was wearing a long cape with red stars and ribbons.

"Ahem!," she said in a shy voice. "Ladies and gentlemen, please step this way!"

Mother and Father rose to their feet. "What's going on?" Father whispered.

"Quiet, please." said Polly.

The bedroom had been transformed into a stage! Two large sheets had been draped like curtains across the room, and there were two chairs in front of them.

“Take your seats,” said Polly, and then she sat down on the floor beside her mother.

Suddenly there was a loud clanging and the curtains were drawn back to reveal Harry and Baby playing the saucepan-drums. They were dressed in capes and hats.

Then Susan swept onto the stage in a long, shiny dress. "Ladies and gentlemen!" she announced. "I present to you the most fabulous magician in the world - William the Wondrous!"

Mother and Father clapped loudly and William leaped onto the stage. He was dressed like a magician with a large top hat in his hand.

"For my first trick," he cried, "I shall pull some magic streamers out of my hat!"

He took off his hat, put in his hand, and pulled out a string of multicoloured handkerchiefs tied together with big knots.

"Hurray!" cried Mother and Father, and William the Wondrous bowed.

William did several more marvellous tricks, with Susan's help, and Baby did lots of drum-rolls on the saucepans.

Meanwhile, Harry had disappeared behind the curtains....

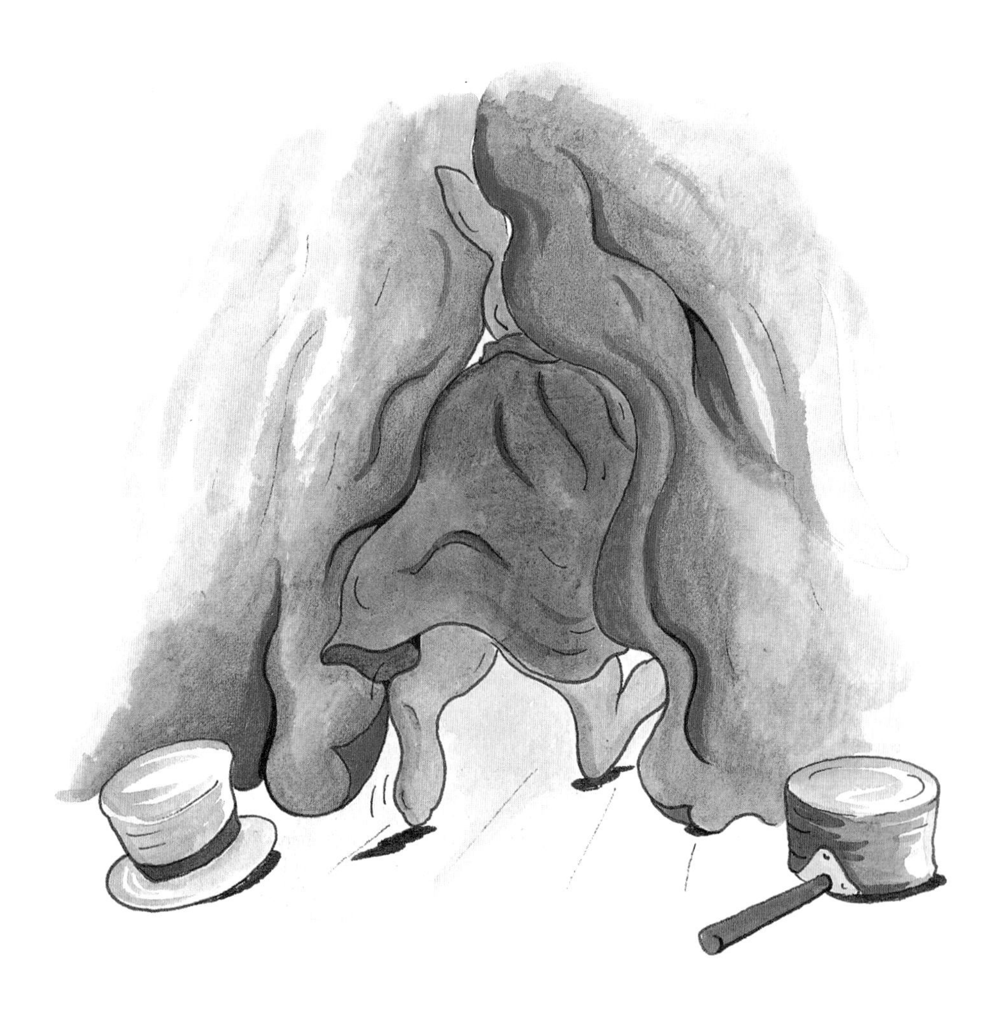

"And now," said William the Wondrous, "my last and greatest piece of magic. Prepare to be amazed!"

Mother and Father watched in great anticipation as Susan and William pushed a large heavy box onto the stage. It was brightly decorated with moons and stars.

"This is the magic doubling box," explained William the Wondrous. "I shall now put one handsome rabbit into the box, and turn him into two handsome rabbits!"

The audience drew it's breath.

"Would Harry the Handsome please come onto the stage!" cried the magician.

Harry walked onto the stage. He looked very dignified and smart. He and William shook hands.

"Now step into the box," said William. "And try not to be afraid."

Harry stepped carefully into the box.

Father thought he heard someone say "Ouch!" and there was a scuffle inside the box as Harry disappeared.

Then Susan put on the lid.

"Let the magic begin!" cried William the Wondrous. He tapped the box twice and then turned around three times and sang a string of magical words.

Even Susan, Polly and Baby were excited and they had seen the trick before!

"Where there was one rabbit, let there now be two!" cried William. The lid of the box burst open and two identical rabbits leaped out!

Of course Mother and Father knew perfectly well that it was just the twins, Harry and Tom. But it really did look as if William had turned one rabbit into two rabbits! They clapped and cheered and all the children came rushing over.

"Weren't we clever!" they shouted. "Did you enjoy our show?" They laughed until their sides were splitting.

The Bunnykins told all their friends about the magic show, and soon everyone in Little Twitching wanted to see William the Wondrous perform his doubling trick.

Mother and Father Bunnykins were very proud of their children!

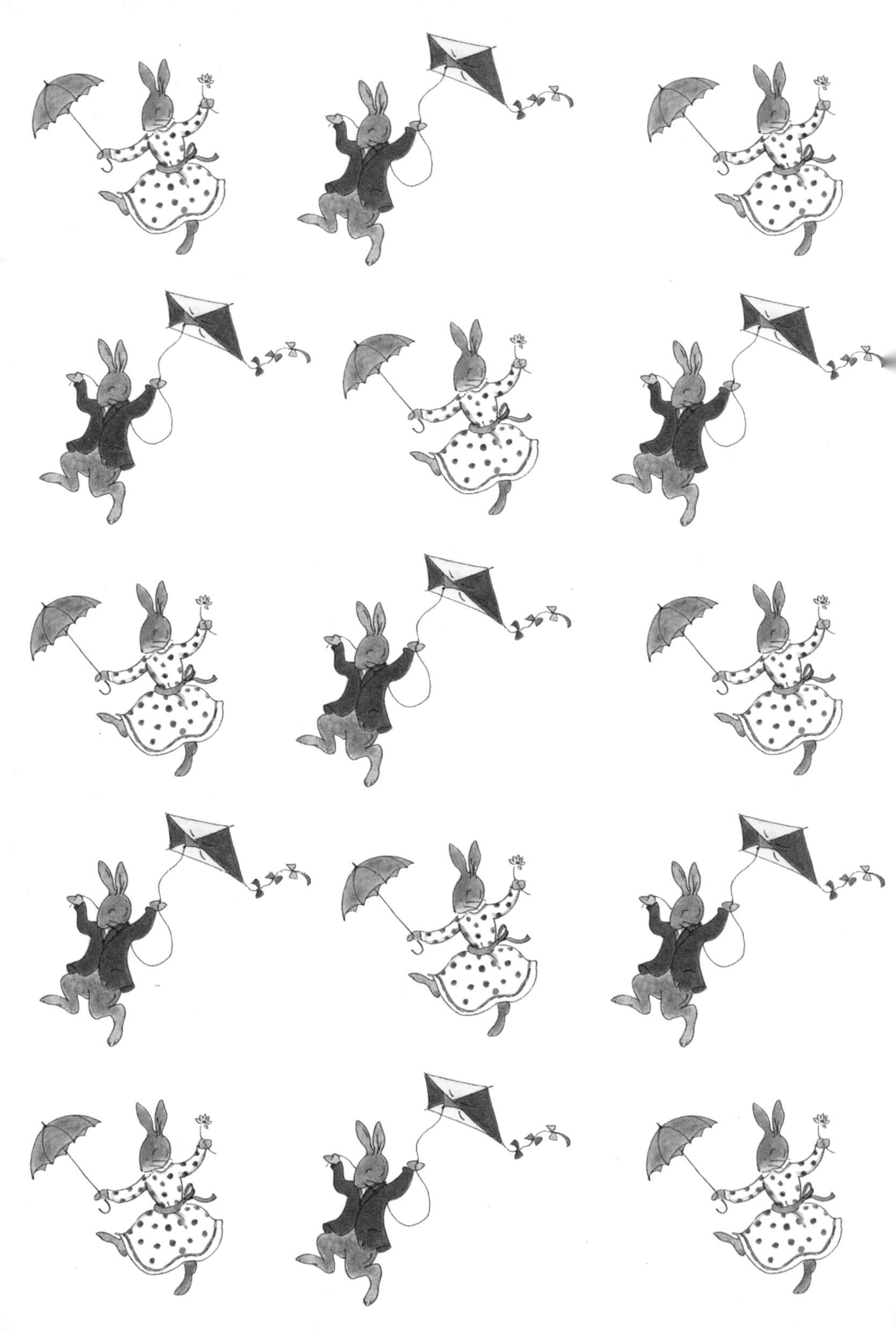